For Oscar and Sara,
Staś and Jagoda

Jan and David would like to thank
Lois Bülow-Osborne, Kate Davies,
Paula MacDonald, and Denise Johnstone-Burt
for their invaluable help and encouragement.

Text copyright © 2014 by David Walser
Illustrations copyright © 2014 by Jan Pieńkowski

First U.S. edition 2014

Library of Congress Catalog Card Number 2013955675
ISBN 978-0-7636-7320-8

14 15 16 17 18 19 SCP 10 9 8 7 6 5 4 3 2 1

Printed in Humen, Dongguan, China

This book was typeset in Golden Type and Fairytale.
The illustrations were done in mixed media.

Candlewick Press
99 Dover Street
Somerville, Massachusetts 02144

visit us at www.candlewick.com

Jan Pieńkowski

The Glass Mountain

Tales from Poland

retold by David Walser

CANDLEWICK PRESS

Contents

David and Jan in Warsaw, winter 1981

Foreword
by David Walser

This is the fourth book of fairy tales that Jan and I have worked on together. The others involved translating and retelling stories from German and French, but since I do not speak or read Polish, this book had to be approached differently. First I read every English version of classic Polish tales I could lay my hands on. There are many, and I marveled at how dissimilar the various tellings are. There are so many accounts, for instance, of Pan Twardowski's colorful life that he could be made to sound either thoroughly unpleasant and deserving of his punishment or else beleaguered by his difficult, nagging wife.

Then I had the great advantage of Jan telling me how he remembered these stories from his childhood and translating some of them orally as he read them in Polish. I would always wait a day or two before writing them down in my own words. Since no two versions were the same, I felt no embarrassment in adding elements from my own imagination when it seemed appropriate. For instance, I introduced the Hejnał trumpeter's grandson in "The Trumpeter of Kraków."

In most countries, fairy tales favor dragons. In these tales from Poland, dragons become so believable that you think they must have existed. In addition, the Devil often gets more than a walk-on part and always has the best tunes.

My Polish Childhood
by Jan Pieńkowski

I was born in Warsaw, but my first memory is from my father's country house, which stood next to the River Bug in the northeast of Poland. I remember refusing to let my nanny push my tricycle and insisting on doing it myself, however clumsily. I lived in the countryside throughout the Second World War, and, since Polish schools were all closed during the war, my parents were my principal teachers.

But there was another source of education: the stories that the lady next door, Pani Kobuszewska, would tell me each afternoon.

Photo taken by my father, with my mother and our horses, winter 1941

She was given the task of persuading me to drink milk every day. When I had milk in our dairy, straight from our cow, I loved it, but my mother was the daughter of a doctor, so she insisted it ought to be boiled. Pani Kobuszewska hit on the idea of telling me stories: she would stop on a cliff-hanger every so often, just as Shahrazade did when she told her husband the stories of *A Thousand and One Nights.* I had to take a gulp of horrid hot milk before she would continue. In this way I heard the whole canon of Polish folktales. The scary heroine of some of these stories, the witch Baba Jaga, soon came to haunt me at bedtime. Fortunately I could see the light seeping under the door and hear my parents' voices. They, of course, did not realize that Pani Kobuszewska had played her Shahrazade role that same afternoon.

The other household activity that was to leave its mark on my

With an orphaned fox cub, found starving in the woods

work was the annual visit of a countrywoman who came to make new "curtains" for the kitchen windows. She took sheets of heavy white paper, and, using a pair of shears, she cut out a lively network of birds, flowers, and human figures. These were then glued to the window frames like lace curtains until her next visit. There was only one pair of shears in the house, so she had to wait until the sheep had been shorn before she could make the curtains. She never repeated her patterns, and her dexterity with the shears made a terrific impression on me.

My next lesson in paper-cutting was in Warsaw in 1944, during the Warsaw Uprising, a sixty-three-day battle between the Polish Home Army and the German occupying troops. When the bombing began, my mother took me to the cellar along with all the other mothers and children. It was rather boring, but one of the soldiers came down to have a rest and a nap. When he woke up, he found a pair of scissors and started cutting out little paper figures to amuse us children. He spread out each animal's legs so they all stood up like a little zoo. I was mesmerized and forgot about the bombing.

Paper cutouts are a form of Polish folk art, and eventually I started cutting out paper figures myself. All the figures in this book are cut out with scissors and pinking shears.

Say It in Polish

Polish word	How to say it	English meaning
Baba Jaga	BAH-bah YAH-gah	name of a legendary witch
Hejnał	HAY-now	hourly bugle call
Jan Pieńkowski	yahn pyen-KOF-skee	name (Jan means John)
Jurek	YOO-rek	name (George)
Kazik	KAH-jik	name (a nickname of Casimir)
Kościół Mariacki	KOSH-choo mah-ree-aht-skee	Church of Saint Mary
Kraków	KRAH-koof	former capital city of Poland
Maciek	MAHT-chek	name (Matthew)
Pan Twardowski	pahn tfar-DOF-skee	name (Pan means "Mr.")
Paweł	PAH-vel	name (Paul)
pierogi	pyeh-ROG-ee	dumplings
Staś	stash	name (a nickname of Stanislaus)
Wanda	VAHN-dah	name (Wanda)
Warszawa	var-SHAH-vah	Warsaw, capital city of Poland
Wawel	VAH-vel	castle complex in Kraków
Wiola	vee-YOLL-ah	name (Viola)
Wisła	VIS-wa	Vistula, a river in Poland
Zosia	ZOH-shah	name (Sophia)

The Fern Flower

On Midsummer's Day, the whole of Bogdan's village turned out as usual to celebrate. They built a huge bonfire, and young and old were getting ready to dance the night away. But not Bogdan: his mother had told him the legend of the fern flower.

"If you find it on Midsummer's Night before the first cockcrow, you will become the richest person in the village," she said. "But beware! You will not be able to share your riches with anyone else. If you do, you will lose everything."

Bogdan did not let that worry him. Before sunset, he said good-bye to his dog, Pavel, told his mother where he was going, and plunged into the forest.

Soon the well-worn paths had disappeared and Bogdan was forcing his way through thick undergrowth that tore at his clothes and scratched his skin. He had been brought up on tales of evil spirits who lived deep in the forest, and he imagined that there were eyes staring at him from among the trees. He jumped at every unexpected sound.

Bogdan could no longer hear the revelry back in his village or see the comforting glow of the bonfire. He was growing tired when he came to a clearing among the trees that was thick with ferns.

This is the very place to find the magic flower, he thought, and at that moment he saw a glow of white. He knew immediately that he had found what he was looking for. He rushed forward and picked the fern flower—but as he did so, he heard the distant sound of a cock crowing. He was too late!

The brilliant white flower wilted and fell from his hand, and wailings and mad laughter filled the air. He fainted and fell to the ground.

Bogdan's poor mother waited up all night, growing more and more distressed. When there was no sign of him by morning, she asked her neighbors to help find him. Even though they had been up most of the night dancing and drinking, they reluctantly agreed. They walked and they walked, they called and they hollered, but they couldn't find Bogdan anywhere.

Then, just as they
were about to give up, they
came across someone lying
unconscious, half concealed
by branches. It was Bogdan!

They tried waking him
without success, so the strongest
man among them hoisted him
onto his back and carried him all
the way home.

Bogdan soon recovered and the
following year, on Midsummer's Day,
he told his mother he was going to try his
luck for a second time. She did her best to
dissuade him but he had made up his mind:
he wanted to be the richest man in the village.

Again he set out around sunset and walked
until he was completely exhausted, his clothes
in tatters. Just as he had decided to give up, he
stumbled on a clearing thick with ferns and saw
the glow of the fern flower.

Alas! It was too late: he heard the cock crow.
There was a flash of lightning and a roll of thunder,
and dreadful cackling filled the air.

He fell down unconscious once more.

When Bogdan failed to return
the next day, his mother pleaded
with her neighbors to help
search for him again.
They remembered
only too well
what a long
and difficult
search it
had
been
the
previous
year, but
they agreed.

After hours
of fruitless searching,
when they were about to
turn back, they found him
lying unconscious amid the ferns.

Another year passed, and
Bogdan decided to look for the fern
flower one more time. He set off much
earlier, so that by the time it was dark, he was
already well into the forest. And yes! Just before
midnight, he stumbled on a clearing filled with ferns.

When he saw the familiar glow of white, he rushed forward to pick the magic flower.

Flashes lit up the clearing, hail poured from the heavens, and demonic laughter filled his ears, but he held on tightly to the flower, pressing it to his chest until the sound and fury ceased. A huge crack opened in the earth in front of him, and his eyes were dazzled by the glint of gold and silver coins. He knew that he had found the riches he so wanted.

Bogdan was now indeed the wealthiest man in the village. He built himself a large mansion and hired servants to cater to his every wish. His coachman drove him about in a splendid carriage.

At first his new life seemed exciting: by day he ate the tastiest foods and walked in his garden, admiring the dazzling flowers. By night he slept between the smoothest linen sheets in a four-poster bed. But he soon grew bored. He tried to forget his mother and his beloved dog, but he could not get them out of his mind. He missed his mother's cooking and the welcome his dog gave him whenever he returned home. One moment he would decide to go and see

them, but the next he would remind himself, *If I try to share my wealth with my poor mother, I shall lose everything. Then how shall I survive? She knows how to support herself, but if I were suddenly penniless, I would have no idea how to earn a living.*

One day he could bear it no longer. He called the coachman and set out for his old home. When they arrived, he could see that the cottage had fallen into disrepair: rusty tools lay abandoned in the long grass, and there was a broken windowpane in his old bedroom. He left his carriage and walked toward the gate where his dog, now old, lay on the path in the sun. "Pavel!" he said softly, but the dog did not even raise its head.

As he walked toward the front door, his mother, now grown frail, came out to see who had arrived in such a magnificent carriage.

He was moved almost to tears to see his mother's threadbare dress and called out, "Mother! It's me!" but there was not even a flicker of recognition in her eyes.

Bogdan turned and shouted to the coachman, "Drive home!"

Months passed, but Bogdan could no longer sleep. He decided he had to help his old mother before it was too late, so he went back to the cottage. As he approached the front door, one of his old neighbors came up to him.

"Where is my dog?" demanded Bogdan.

"Your dog is dead," said the man sharply, "and your mother is ill in bed."

Bogdan rushed up to the gate, ready to give his mother all the coins in his pocket, but then he stopped abruptly.

My poor mother may not live long, but I am still young, he thought. *How will I survive without money?* He turned on his heel and drove back to his mansion.

Bogdan felt so guilty that a few weeks later, he finally became determined to risk everything to help his mother. This time, when his carriage stopped in front of the cottage, his old home was in ruins. All the windowpanes had been broken, the garden gate hung on one hinge, and weeds covered the path.

He pushed open the front door and called out timidly, "Mother, are you there?" but there was no reply.

He walked all through the house, which smelled of damp and decay, but it was empty. He stumbled out into the sunlight again and found his old neighbor standing at the gate, looking at him.

"You're too late!" said the man curtly. "Your mother is dead."

Bogdan turned away. He cursed himself with a bitter oath. As he did so, the earth opened in front of him and swallowed both him and the fern flower, which he still kept in his tunic next to his heart.

The Kraków Dragon

Prince Krak lived in Wawel Castle, on the banks of the River Vistula, with his beautiful daughter, Princess Zosia. He was a kind and generous ruler and kept in touch with everything that was going on in his kingdom, so when he heard that sheep were disappearing every night from the fields around the city, he was very concerned.

One morning the Captain of the Guard announced, "A shepherd to see you, sire! He says it's very urgent."

"Show him in!" replied the prince without hesitation.

The shepherd entered the room and took a parcel from under his cloak. He tore off the wrapping, revealing a blood-stained leather shoe with the foot still in it.

"What on earth have you got there?" asked the prince.

"Sire, it's all that's left of my friend," said the shepherd. "He went out last night to guard our flock. He told me he wanted to catch the sheep thief red-handed. When he didn't return this morning, I went looking for him, and found only this. . . ."

His voice tailed off and tears rolled down his cheeks as he held out his friend's shoe.

"Sit down, sit down!" said the kindly prince. "Things are more serious than I thought. It is not a thief we are dealing with but a dangerous animal."

At that moment, the captain appeared again. "Jurek, the basket maker's apprentice to see you, sire!" he said.

"Show him in!" said the Prince.

The young man entered in a state of great agitation. "What news do you bring?" asked Prince Krak.

"Sire," he replied, "I was down by the river this morning, collecting reeds for our baskets, when I looked up and saw a creature lying in front of a cave. Its eyes were shut, its scaly stomach was rising and falling, and its feet were as big as . . . as big as that bowl there," he said, pointing to a huge china bowl on the dresser. "Its claws moved in and out as it breathed, just like my cat's when she's asleep. Then smoke poured out of its nostrils, and I knew it was a dragon! I ran for my life and I didn't stop until I got here, sire."

"You did well to escape!" said Prince Krak, turning to the Captain of the Guard.

"Captain," he ordered, "send your bravest soldiers to kill this terrible dragon. Young Jurek here will show you the way. I shall give my daughter's hand in marriage to the man who succeeds in ridding us of this monster."

Jurek led the soldiers to the cave but hid in the bushes while they crept in to fight the dragon. After just a few moments, he heard a terrible roaring, followed by bloodcurdling screams. Smoke belched out of the cave's mouth. Silence followed. Jurek waited no longer. He ran back to tell the prince what had happened.

In the days that followed, many brave knights went to the cave to try to kill the dragon. None returned. So the prince decided he must go himself. He summoned his armorer.

"Make me a suit of armor so strong that not even a dragon could bite through it, and choose me the best and sharpest sword you have!" he ordered.

As soon as the armor was made, Prince Krak struggled into it, but it was so heavy that he feared that he would be exhausted by the time he reached the dragon. At that moment, the captain knocked again.

"Another fellow to see you, sire," he said. "It's young Maciek, the cobbler's apprentice. He says he has urgent news about the dragon."

"Show him in, then!" said the prince impatiently. The captain brought the young man in.

"What do YOU want, Maciek?" said the prince irritably. "Can't you see I am very busy at the moment?"

"Yes, sire," said Maciek, "but I've found a way to kill the dragon without risking your life."

Prince Krak looked up. He was already perspiring, and he was not looking forward to the long walk, let alone the fight. He was prepared to grasp at any straw.

"All I need," said Maciek, "is a freshly killed sheep and someone to help me carry it. I can do the rest."

"That doesn't sound like much of a weapon to me. You should be looking for a wife rather than fighting dragons with dead sheep," replied the prince, and he roared with laughter.

"Sire, I am deadly serious," said Maciek. "Give me a chance and I shall rid you of this beast. And, if I succeed, I *shall* find a wife—your beautiful daughter, Zosia."

Prince Krak saw that the young man was not joking. "All right, then," he said. "We shall give you what you want. Jurek can help you carry the sheep."

When Maciek was given the sheep's carcass, he slit open its stomach, scraped out its guts, and filled the cavity with a concoction of tar and sulfur. He was an expert cobbler, so it was easy for him to sew the sheep up again.

Just before dawn, he and Jurek carried the sheep to the cave and propped it up: it looked almost alive. They hid close by and waited and waited and waited and waited . . . until suddenly they heard strange sounds from inside the cave. Moments later, the dragon's head emerged, followed by its hideous, scaly, glistening body. The beast stretched its great jagged wings, yawned, and let out a stream of fire and smoke. It looked down and saw the sheep, then it pounced and swallowed it whole. Maciek and Jurek could see the sheep sliding down the dragon's neck to its belly.

At first the dragon looked pleased, but it soon began to bellow in terrible pain, shaking all over and stamping its feet. Then it spread its mighty wings, stumbled toward the river, and hurled itself into the water.

There was a huge splash, followed by silence. Jurek held on tightly to Maciek, and they both held their breath. An explosion rang out and was heard all over the city. Bits of wings, skin, and limbs were hurled high into the air. An enormous severed foot with five huge spiky claws landed close by,

narrowly

missing

the two

young men.

Maciek and Jurek made their way back to the castle, carrying the foot as their trophy. Prince Krak was delighted to see them again; he had feared the worst when he heard the explosion.

"Whatever have you got there? And what was that loud bang?" asked the prince.

"Sire," replied Maciek, "the dragon swallowed the sheep whole, not knowing I had stuffed its belly with tar and sulfur. The beast must have been in agony, because it dived into the water and drank until it exploded. And now, sire, I want to ask you for the hand of Princess Zosia!"

"You're a fine young fellow," said the prince, "and I shall be pleased for you to marry my daughter."

The Frog Bride

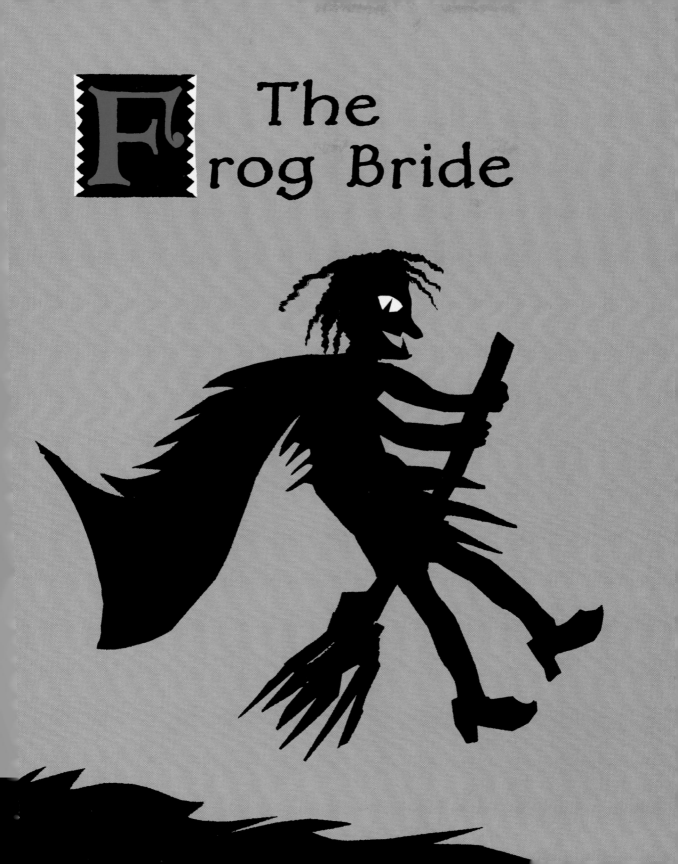

nce upon a time, there was a king whose wife died, leaving him with three sons. When they were all grown up, he said to them, "It is time I appointed my successor, but as you know, the custom is that I must choose an heir who is married. So off you go! Each of you must find a wife, and whoever picks the best wife shall be my heir."

The young men panicked—they had all been busy enjoying themselves and had not thought about settling down with wives and children—so they sought advice from a wise man.

"Stand on the highest tower of the castle with a bow and arrow," he told them. "Each of you must shoot an arrow in a different direction. Where the arrow lands, you will find the young woman to marry."

The eldest brother fired his arrow toward the part of town where the wealthy people lived. In the house where the arrow fell, he met a lovely young lady who was happy to marry him.

The middle brother fired his arrow toward the part of town where the gentry lived. In the house where the arrow fell, he found a lovely young lady who was happy to marry him.

The youngest brother fired his arrow into the countryside beyond the castle walls. When he found it, the arrow was floating in the middle of a pond. He was wondering what to do next when a little green frog crawled onto the arrow and spoke to him.

"Prince," said the little frog, in a charming human voice, "why are you looking so thoughtful?"

The young man could hardly believe his ears. "Well," he replied, after he had gotten over his surprise, "I am wondering where to find the woman I'm going to marry."

"Don't worry!" said the little frog. "I shall be your wife."

The young prince thought he had no choice but to go along with this strange plan. He placed the frog carefully in his pocket and walked back to the castle.

That evening the king sent a message to his sons. "I want each of you to ask your fiancée to weave a rug and bring it to me tomorrow," he said.

The youngest prince went to his room and sat by a window, deep in thought.

"Why are you looking so sad, my prince?" asked the little green frog.

The prince told her, and she said, "Don't worry! By morning I shall have a rug for you to take to the king."

As soon as the prince had left the room, the little frog climbed onto the windowsill and sang:

"Gentle breezes blow my way;
    Bring me all I need today
    To weave a rug to please our king."

Down the rays of the setting sun came angels bearing colored threads, flowers, and gold dust from the deepest seas. They flew into the room and set to work.

As the sun rose, the little frog handed her prince the rolled-up rug. "Take this to the king, my dearest!" she said.

The eldest prince was the first to roll out his fiancée's rug in front of the king. It portrayed lots of expensive and desirable objects set out on a rich blue background. The king gazed at it and was delighted.

Then it was the middle prince's turn. His fiancée's rug showed her family's splendid coat of arms against a rich red background. The king saw it and was so delighted that he could not decide which of the two rugs was the best.

When the youngest prince rolled out his fiancée's rug next to those of his brothers, the king gasped. Lifelike flowers appeared to spring out of a field of ravishing colors, all dusted with gold.

"This is what I call a rug!" said the king. There could be no doubt in anyone's mind as to who had won the contest.

"But there's one more task," said the king. "Ask your fiancées each to make pierogi and bring them to me tomorrow for my breakfast."

Once again the young prince returned to his room and sat down by the window with a worried look on his face.

"What troubles you now, my princeling?" asked the little frog.

"The king was really pleased with your rug, dear little frog, but now he has asked for pierogi. I don't know how you wove that wonderful rug, but how can you possibly make pierogi?"

"Go to bed!" said the little frog. "You will have them by morning." Again she summoned help at the window:

"Gentle breezes blow my way;

Bring me all I need today

To make pierogi for our king."

The next morning, she handed the prince delicious-looking pierogi to give the king.

When the king tried his eldest son's pierogi, they were so tasty that he found it difficult not to eat all of them. When he sampled his second son's, he had to remind himself to leave space for some more. Then he bit into his youngest son's pierogi. The flavors were so mouthwatering that he felt quite dizzy and had to lean back in his chair.

"This is what I call perfection!" he exclaimed. "Well, sons, I should now like to meet the young ladies who wove these rugs and made these delicious pierogi."

The youngest prince had no idea what to do. *How can I possibly present the little frog as my bride?* he wondered.

But when he reached his rooms, she seemed to already know his problem.

"It is time, my dear, for me to tell you my secret. I am not what I seem. My mother turned me into a frog when I was a child to protect me from some wicked sorcerers. Now you shall see what I really am: a princess."

At that moment, the most beautiful girl the prince had ever seen stepped out of the frog skin. He was overcome with joy as he kissed his fiancée for the first time. "Now, my treasure," he said, "you must get ready to meet the king. We are already late!"

"You go on ahead, my dearest," she said, and she told him how to prepare the king for her entrance.

The two elder brothers brought their fiancées to meet the king. They curtsied and kissed the king's hand, and they were so agreeable and pretty that the king liked them both equally. Then his youngest son appeared alone.

"Where is your fiancée?" asked the king.

"When you hear the wind roar, Father, it will mean she is on her way," he said. "When the lightning flashes, she will be outside, and when the thunder rolls, she will appear."

And so it turned out. Wind rattled the windowpanes, lightning chased away every shadow in the great hall, and thunder rolled like a drumbeat. The princess entered and curtsied to the king. She was so poised and graceful that at first the king was speechless. Then he called his youngest son aside.

"Where did you meet this wonderful girl?" he asked.

The prince told him the whole story.

"Go back to your room immediately and burn that frog skin!" ordered the king. "That is the only way to keep your fiancée."

The prince rushed back and found the shriveled frog skin on the carpet. He threw it on the fire and watched as it writhed and hissed before burning up and disappearing.

Later that evening, when the princes and their fiancées went back to their rooms, the princess asked, "But where is my frog skin?"

"I burned it, my love," replied the young prince.

The princess grew agitated. "The frog skin was my only protection," she wailed. "What will keep me safe now?"

He watched in horror as she began to melt before his eyes into other creatures: first a cat, then a rabbit, and then a little duck, which flew straight out of the window and disappeared into the night.

The prince was distraught. He set off immediately to find her and walked for days across snowy mountains, deep valleys, fertile plains, and deserts, but to no avail. Then one day, while walking through a field, he saw the strangest house he'd ever seen — it stood, quite literally, on a chicken's leg. He called out, "Is anyone there?"

With little hops, the house turned to face him, then the door opened and he heard a voice call, "Come in!" When he entered, he saw Baba Jaga, the witch he had heard about since he was a child, sitting by the fire.

"Sit down!" said the fearsome witch. He did as he was told; she looked like someone it was better not to cross.

"What are you doing here, young man?" asked Baba Jaga. The prince was so depressed and tired from his fruitless travels that he told her the whole story. Baba Jaga looked at him. "Since you told me the truth, I shall help you," she said. "Your fiancée comes here every day. When she flies in, you must catch her and hold on to her through thick and thin. That will prove your loyalty to her."

Baba Jaga covered the prince with her cloak just in time. There was a "Quack! Quack!" at the window, and a beautiful little duck landed on the sill. The prince crept out from under the cloak and caught hold of her.

She began to struggle immediately. She changed into a rabbit that kicked him, then an eagle that pecked him, then a snake that hissed at him. The prince held on tightly until the snake changed back into a duck. The duck grew calmer, and then quite suddenly it changed back into his beautiful fiancée. Only then did the prince let go.

He kissed her tenderly. "I shall not change again," said his beloved, "for now I know you will truly care for me and protect me against danger."

They said good-bye to Baba Jaga, thanking her a million times, and made their way back to the castle, where the king was waiting anxiously for them. He wept with pleasure when they entered.

"Welcome home, my children!" he said. "You shall be my heirs. I know my kingdom will be in good hands."

The Miller's Daughters

There was once a miller who lived in a small village on the banks of the River Vistula. He had three daughters, Magda, Viola, and Wanda, and he wanted to teach them to read, but he could not afford three sets of lessons. He knew that if he favored one daughter above the rest, there would be jealousy and resentment, so sadly he gave up the idea.

One day a woman came to his mill begging for something to eat. The miller took pity on her, invited her in, sat her by the fire, and gave her a plate of food. While she was eating, she pulled out a book and started to read. The miller had an idea.

"Would you be prepared to teach my daughters to read? You could stay here and share our food," he said.

"Certainly! I would be happy to teach them. In fact in better times, I used to be a teacher," she answered with a smile.

The teacher was eager to start right away, so they arranged for Magda, the eldest, to begin her lessons the very next morning. But Magda was only interested in clothes and makeup. She wanted to capture the most eligible husband, and she spent a lot of time looking at herself in the mirror. The teacher waited and waited for Magda to turn up, but the girl never made it: she simply had to go and buy a hat.

The next day, the teacher was ready to work with Viola, but Viola thought of little else but dancing and music. She forgot about her lesson because there was a dance in the next village that she simply had to attend.

The following day it was Wanda's turn, and she couldn't wait. She had three books by her bed, and every night she sniffed the handsome leather bindings and turned the pages lovingly, looking at the pictures and wondering what secrets the words held.

After her lesson, Wanda picked up a book and ran to her father.

"Chapter one," she read out with pride. Her father was thrilled.

And so it went on. Magda and Viola always had some excuse for missing their lessons. Wanda, on the other hand, was ready for every lesson and was soon reading fluently.

One day a wealthy-looking man came to the village. People whispered that he was looking for a wife, so Magda put on her most elegant frock and bumped into him—quite by accident, of course! It was not long before the man asked the miller if he could marry Magda. The miller was delighted to marry off his eldest daughter to a rich man, so he agreed.

But sadly this man was not what he seemed: he was, in fact, a wicked magician.

As soon as they were married, the magician whisked his young wife away to his castle. She wandered around the corridors, gazing into the grand rooms filled with beautiful clothes, musical instruments, and books.

"Have a good time trying on the dresses," said the magician. "I have some business to do in the next village, but I will be back soon. You may go anywhere you like in the castle—except that little room at the end of the corridor. You must not go there!"

Once the magician had left, Magda ran around the castle, trying on one amazing dress after another. But it was not long before she grew bored.

I wonder what is in that little room, she thought. *I'm sure it wouldn't matter if I had a peek.* And so she did. She turned the handle very slowly and pulled the door open a fraction.

A hairy hand
shot out and pulled her
inside. Magda screamed and
burst into tears, but when she
looked around, there was no one to
be seen. On one side of the room there
were shelves of musty old books, and on the
other side were rows of birdcages. Some of the
cages were empty, and some contained miserable-
looking yellow birds.

When the magician returned, he called for his young
wife, but there was no reply. So he opened the door to the
forbidden room. He found Magda crouching, terrified, in a corner.

"You have disobeyed me," he said, "and I shall punish you." He
spoke some words Magda did not understand, and she immediately
turned into a little yellow bird. The magician snatched her up and
pushed her into an empty cage.

The next day, the magician returned to the village. Viola and Wanda were overjoyed to see Magda's husband.

"Why have you not brought our sister with you?" they asked.

"Come with me and you shall see her," he replied.

Wanda did not want to miss her reading lesson, so Viola went off alone with the magician. When they arrived at the castle, the magician said that Magda was looking at a new dress and would be back any minute.

"Make yourself at home," he said to Viola. "You can play with the musical instruments and go anywhere you like . . . except into that room at the end of the passage. Don't go in there!"

Viola entertained herself by trying out the unfamiliar instruments, but there was no one to dance with and she soon grew bored.

I wonder what is in that little room, she thought. *I'm sure it wouldn't matter if I had a peek.*

She opened the door a crack, and a hairy hand shot out and
pulled her into the room. She screamed, but no one came, so she
stopped and looked around her. All she could see were books and
birdcages, some of them with miserable-looking yellow birds inside.
When the magician returned, he turned her into a little yellow bird
and stuffed her into another empty cage.

The following day, the magician went back to the miller's house.

"Where are my sisters?" asked Wanda.

"They are waiting for you at my castle," said the magician. "Why don't you come and see them? I've got some interesting books for you to read. Then you and Viola can go back home together."

Her father was milling wheat that day, so off she went without saying good-bye.

When they reached the castle, the magician said to Wanda, "Wait here while I fetch your sisters. Make yourself at home and explore my book collection. You may go anywhere you like — except into that room at the end of the passage."

Like her sisters, Wanda eventually grew bored, so she peeked into the forbidden room and was dragged in. But unlike her sisters, Wanda could read. When she had recovered from the shock, she saw that the books on the shelves were all about magic. She took down one called *How to Make Spells* and began to read.

Before long, she heard footsteps approaching: *Clomp, clomp! Clomp, clomp!*

The door flew open — it was the magician. But just as he was about to cast his spell, Wanda said in a firm voice,

"Abracadabra!

Curse this house.

Turn this man

Into a mouse!"

The magician shriveled up before her eyes and became a little squeaking mouse.

Wanda snatched him up and thrust him into an empty cage. Then she turned to the little yellow birds and said:

"Abracadabra! Free these birds!

Turn them back to what they were."

The yellow birds burst out of their cages and became people again. Wanda spotted her two sisters among them. They hugged her and cried on her shoulder.

As everyone was leaving to go home, Wanda picked up the cage with the mouse in it.

"You are coming with me, Mr. Magician," she said.

I'm sad to say, Wanda had a very greedy cat. After a day or two, it found a way to open the door of the cage and had a tasty meal. All it left was the mouse's tail!

azik thought his grandfather had the best job in the world: he was one of the trumpeters that played the Hejnał from the top of the Kościół Mariacki Tower at dawn and at dusk. Sometimes his grandfather also kept watch through the night, in case the city was attacked by the fierce Tartar warriors who roamed the countryside. Kazik wanted to follow in his grandfather's footsteps and become a Hejnał trumpeter when he grew up.

One morning, as dawn was breaking, Kazik awoke with a start. He could hear the Hejnał being played over and over again. At first he was so sleepy that he couldn't make sense of it. Then he remembered his grandfather was on duty that night on the Mariacki Tower—he must be warning the citizens about an attack.

The tune stopped abruptly, midway through a note. Without further ado, Kazik jumped out of bed, threw on some clothes, and rushed out of the house. He raced along the street, second right, first left into the Market Square, around the Town Hall, and up the stairs of the tower two at a time. As he entered the lookout room at the top, he saw his grandfather lying on the floor with an arrow through his throat.

From one of the openings in the tower, he could see a horde of men galloping about in the morning mist at the foot of the city walls.

They had to be the Tartars he had been told about so often. Then he had an idea. He picked up his grandfather's trumpet and put it to his lips. The Hejnał sang out again over the city. Again and again he played the tune! When at last he stopped, exhausted, he watched the townsfolk rushing from every quarter to defend the walls. By this time, the Tartars were firing so many arrows they looked like flocks of starlings coming over the battlements. Some of the townsfolk were firing back at the Tartars; others were striking them with swords as they reached the tops of ladders placed against the walls.

Kazik sat down by his grandfather's side. For the first time, tears rolled down his cheeks.

Moments later, a priest entered the room. He looked at the dead man on the floor and at Kazik, and he understood what had happened.

"You have done well, son," he said. "I think we will hold off this attack, and it's all thanks to your grandfather spotting the Tartars in time, and to both of you playing the Hejnał. You shall be one of the Hejnał trumpeters as soon as you are old enough."

Nowadays the Hejnał is played every day on the hour, every hour, to all the four winds, by a live trumpeter. The trumpeter always stops abruptly on the note that Kazik's grandfather was playing when he died.

The Glass Mountain

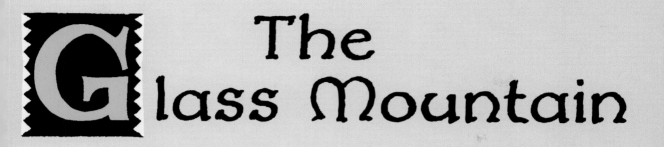

everyone knew it as the Glass Mountain. It rose up steeply from behind the village, and at the top of its slippery, shiny-as-glass slopes, an eerie castle stood out against the sky. It was no ordinary castle: it was enchanted, and the beautiful princess who lived there was also under a spell.

You might think the princess would be happy, because the rooms of the castle were filled with treasure: rubies, diamonds, and sapphires, and enough gold and silver coins to satisfy anyone. But she was not happy; she was no better than a prisoner. The castle was guarded by a fearsome dragon, and an eagle swooped about, ready to attack anyone who dared to approach. In order to reach the princess, you would have to scale the mountain, overcome the eagle, pick golden apples from the tree by the castle entrance, and feed them to the dragon.

The princess knew that there were young noblemen eager to marry her; they were forever attempting to ride up the slippery mountain on horseback. She watched them from her window, praying they would succeed, but as each of them slipped to his death, she was left to mourn again.

"Will I ever have anyone to love and to share all these riches with?" she asked as she gazed sadly out her window.

In the village below the mountain, there lived a blacksmith's apprentice named Leon. He had watched suitor after suitor try to reach the castle on horseback. Some almost made it to the top, but again and again they fell to their deaths. He hated that each time one of them failed, his horse was also killed. Then one day he had an idea.

Suppose I try to climb the mountain on foot? he thought. *It will be long and difficult because it's so slippery, but I could use the claws of a wild beast to catch in the crevices. Yes! That is how I'll reach the princess!*

Snow fell during the day, so that very evening, Leon went into the forest with his bow and arrow. He found a set of freshly made footprints and followed them until they stopped at the foot of a tree. When he looked up his eyes met those of a large lynx on a branch above him. Slowly he lifted his bow and pulled back the arrow, then fired. The animal fell dead at his feet. He cut off its paws with their wicked, razor-sharp claws and attached them to his own hands and boots. Then he wiped his knife and put it back in his belt before setting off for the mountain.

At first the sky was clear, but as he climbed higher, clouds covered the sun and snow began to fall again. Gradually he became exhausted, until, not far from the summit, he could go no farther. He jammed his lynx claws into some cracks and tried to rest.

A whirring and flapping awoke him. He was just in time to see
the eagle spreading its wings above his head as it sank its claws into
his shoulders. In desperation he grabbed the eagle's legs, and the
mighty bird rose up, dragging him with it. They were heading in the
direction of the castle.

Just as Leon was thinking of the fearsome dragon that would
be waiting for him, he noticed that they were passing right over the

golden apple tree. He reached for his knife, hacked off the eagle's legs, and fell like a stone into the branches of the apple tree. He lay stunned as he watched the bird soar up into the air with agonized cries before plunging to its death far below.

When Leon had recovered his senses, he picked as many golden apples as he could fit into his pockets. Then, as he was climbing down from the tree, he heard a roaring sound that chilled him to the marrow.

It was the dragon, moving awkwardly
but swiftly toward him, like a giant
lizard with horrendous flapping wings.

Fire and smoke shot out of the dragon's
mouth. For a moment, Leon was frozen with
panic, but then he remembered the apples he
was carrying. He lobbed one at the dragon. To his
amazement, the beast caught the apple and swallowed
it. Leon threw another one into its cavernous jaws. The
creature swallowed it, folded its wings, and slipped quietly
into the castle moat.

At that moment, the princess, hearing the commotion,
rushed out across the drawbridge. She saw a handsome young
man coming toward her with a pair of eagle's legs sticking out of his
shoulders. Without a thought for her own safety, she went up to him
and gently extracted the claws. She placed pieces of golden apple on
the wounds and, to his amazement, Leon felt the pain slip away. The
two young people found themselves staring into each other's eyes.

Leon kissed the princess and thanked her for healing him, and with that first kiss, the princess was freed. With their arms around each other, Leon and the princess looked down toward the village and saw people milling about. The princess called the castle messenger by blowing on a silver trumpet. A graceful swallow appeared.

"Fly down to the village and find out what is happening!" said the princess.

The swallow returned to say that the suitors and their horses were coming back to life and setting off for their homes, and that some of the villagers were climbing the mountain, for this was no longer a difficult thing to do. The princess and Leon went to meet them at the castle gates as they arrived.

"You are all invited to our wedding!" they told them.

On their way back to the castle, they passed by the golden apple tree. There, in the topmost branch, sat the eagle, happily pecking at the golden apples.

The eagle never bothered anyone again. The dragon stayed in the moat, coming up now and then when a visitor threw him an apple, and the young couple lived happily ever after.

Pan Twardowski

an Twardowski was a wealthy nobleman who lived in a fine house off Market Square in the center of Kraków. He was very knowledgeable about all sorts of subjects and people often went to him for advice, but Pan Twardowski was not satisfied with his life. He began to dabble in the black arts, and he dreamed of changing base metals into gold and becoming fabulously wealthy—in fact, he was desperate to discover the secret.

One day he decided he could wait no longer. Shortly before midnight, he left his house on foot to meet someone he knew could help him. When he reached the outskirts of the city, he left the path and walked toward a lonely place surrounded by trees. The moon was full, and by its light he saw a mysterious figure, wrapped in a long cloak, coming toward him. As the figure got closer, Pan Twardowski could see horns at each side of his head. It was the Devil—the very person he had come to meet.

"What do you want from me?" asked the Devil.

"I want to have unlimited knowledge and power," Pan Twardowski replied in a level voice.

"Only I have these powers," replied the Devil. "I could lend them to you for a time—but do you know what I must have in return?"

"Yes! My soul! And you shall have it, on one condition: that you can only collect it when I am in Rome."

The Devil laughed and produced a sheet of parchment and a pen from under his cloak. "Then let us sign this contract," he said. He cut a nick in his skin, dipped his pen in his own blood, and signed. Pan Twardowski did the same.

"We are agreed," said the Devil. "But, remember, it won't be long before I collect on my side of the bargain."

The Devil turned on his heel, and Pan Twardowski caught a glimpse of his tail sticking out from under his cloak, glinting in the moonlight. The Devil melted into the trees and disappeared.

Armed with his new powers, Pan Twardowski set to work. He soon became even better known and richer than before. His favorite way of traveling about the countryside was riding on a cockerel the size of a horse: this allowed him to cover large distances in no time at all.

Once at dinner with friends, he conjured up a huge rock in the garden to impress the other guests; it is still there to this day. He could make old people look young again, and on one occasion he even helped the king get one last glimpse of his wife, the queen, who had recently died.

At first he was satisfied with tricks like these, but over time he began to do less pleasant things. When a friend told him about an argument he'd had with someone who lived near Kraków, Pan Twardowski lifted his glass until it caught the sun, and looked toward the man's house. The house suddenly burst into flames and burned to the ground. He tricked a young woman, a potter by trade, into marrying him. When she refused to be an obedient wife, he took his revenge by getting his rowdy friends to destroy all the pots that she was selling at the market.

Not even Pan Twardowski's faithful servant was safe. When he tried to earn a little money on the side by using his master's powers to make an old man young again, Pan Twardowski turned him into a spider, saying, "From now on you will live in a fold of my cloak!"

As news of this kind of behavior spread, people began to be wary of Pan Twardowski, and the Devil grew impatient to receive his side of the bargain. One day, Pan Twardowski heard that a rich and famous man was ill and had asked for his help. He was always happy to mix with important people, so he went to the address he had been given, an inn in a nearby village.

When he pushed open the door, he was met by ear-splitting laughter and demons whirling about in the air. As he paused on the doorstep, the demons settled, and there, lounging in a chair by the fire, was his old acquaintance, the Devil himself.

"You can't do this to me!" Pan Twardowski began to say, but the Devil interrupted him.

"Oh, yes, I can!" he said with a laugh. "Look at the name of this inn." Pan Twardowski glanced at a sign above the door and saw the dreaded word: ROME.

"It's too soon," he said.

But again the Devil broke in: "Not too soon for me, though!"

Pan Twardowski tried every trick he knew to squirm out of his side of the bargain, but the Devil clinched the matter. He reached underneath his cloak and pulled out a document.

"You gave me your word as a gentleman, remember?" he said as he flourished the contract.

Pan Twardowski decided to make one more bid for freedom. He ran to the huge open hearth and climbed up the chimney as fast as he could. When he reached the top, he found himself rising as if by magic into the air, surrounded by circling crows.

He rose higher and higher into the sky until the Rome Inn had disappeared from view and even the city of Kraków was but a speck.

Fortunately he began to regret the wicked things he had done, and he passed his time by singing holy songs. Farmers working in their fields below heard sweet singing from above. God also heard it and took pity on him—and when Pan Twardowski bumped into the moon, he was allowed to stay there.

To this day, if you look very hard at the moon, you might spot Pan Twardowski. His only company is his servant, the spider who still lives in a fold of his cloak. Each month the spider spins a web that lets him all the way down to Kraków. He collects the gossip and returns to relate it to his master. So if you happen to be visiting Kraków, be very careful not to tread on a spider: it might be Pan Twardowski's faithful servant, and you wouldn't want the reformed old trickster to be completely alone, would you?

The **W**arsaw **M**ermaid

One night long ago, two fishermen who lived by the River Vistula heard singing coming from down by the water. When they heard it again the following night, they told their friends about it.

"It must be a mermaid singing," said one of their friends. "Why don't you capture her and take her to the king? He will surely reward you handsomely."

The fishermen liked the idea of a reward, but they were afraid that the mermaid might cast a spell on them. They went to ask the priest for advice.

"Go ahead and catch her!" said the priest. "Make a basket out of willow, then creep up and throw it over her. But be careful to block your ears with wax in case she tries to enchant you with her singing."

The fishermen went home and made a basket as the priest had instructed them, then waited until evening. When they heard the distant sound of sweet singing, they picked up the basket and walked along the riverbank until they caught a glimpse of the mermaid through the reeds. She was a beautiful woman from the waist up, but below the waist, she had the body of a fish, covered in scales that glistened in the moonlight. They quickly stuffed wax into their ears, crept up behind the lovely creature, and flung the basket over her. The poor mermaid moaned and struggled but could not escape.

Since it was now late at night, the fishermen took her to their friend Staś's barn. They asked him to keep her safely locked up for the night, saying they would come back in the morning and take her to the king. Staś agreed, but as soon as the two fishermen had gone home, he went into his barn to take a peek at the mermaid. He could just see her through the basketwork—but he had not thought to block his ears. When the mermaid saw him, she began to sing. It was the most beautiful, sad song he had ever heard.

"Let me go! Let me go, kind man. Let me go back to my home in the river," she pleaded. He could not help himself; he opened up the basket. The mermaid thanked him, slithered toward the riverbank, and disappeared into the gently flowing waters.

Still under her spell, Staś plunged into the water after her, and neither of them was ever seen again.

But the mermaid was not forgotten. Many years later, the little village on the riverbank became the city of Warsaw. You can still see the mermaid on the coat of arms that stands proudly above the entrance to the city, holding a sword in one hand and a shield in the other.

On stormy nights, the wind moans as it blows through the willows along the Warsaw riverbank—or is it the mermaid singing?